Gary Kinsel 93

# Nathan's Christmas

Gary Kriesel

*Illustrated by Mark Fearing*

*Waubesa Press*
*P.O. Box 192*
*Oregon, Wis.*

*To my family and friends, who always believed in me, even when I didn't. . . especially Roxie, Kelly and Jeff.*

**In memory of Jeff Novak**

*Chapter One*

Dinkytown is a town within a town. It is the little community that surrounds the University. The streets are made up of fast food joints, clothing stores, music shops, bookstores, novelty shops and ethnic restaurants. The edges are surrounded by large old houses dotted with "Room for Rent" signs.

The usually busy streets and sidewalks were empty. It was due to more than Christmas break. The snow had fallen and fallen. Dinkytown had been buried in white. The wind whirled the snow in mini-tornados across the empty streets. The airport had been closed for two days, the stores for three. It was the day before Christmas Eve, and the people were just starting to free themselves from the winter storm. There were four people who later would believe the storm was planned. Their lives were changed by the storm and a secret they would hold for the rest of their lives: Nathan.

Sarah lay awake in bed. She was waiting for the bells of the alarm clock to rattle. The alarm clock was like her; old but dependable. She thought that today she had a chance to fool the old thing. She had set the alarm for 4:30 AM, a half hour earlier than her regular time. She knew she would need the extra time because of the snow. The clock was tied to habit just like she was. She would always wake before the alarm went off, lying there and waiting. The minutes were longer then, making her feel she was getting more rest. Sarah knew it was the loneliness. Loneliness caused you to wake up early.

The clock rang with the determination of a

fire alarm, announcing to Sarah, "If you can adjust, so can I!" The clock wore down fast until it was just a "click." She remembered when the clock was new and it would wake the neighbors if someone didn't shut it off. She sometimes had this crazy thought that, if the clock ever died, so would she.

Dressed in her robe and slippers, she went to the kitchen, flicked on the coffee maker and looked out the window to check on the weather. Flakes of snow darted at the garage light. Everything was white. The path to the garbage cans had disappeared, a large branch from the oak tree had fallen to the snow. Sarah sighed. The buses wouldn't be running and that meant she would have to walk the ten blocks to work. Even if she wanted to there was no way she could get the Buick out of the garage. When was the last time she had driven the car? It was three or four years. She had all the reasons to quit driving; buses ran in front of the house, work was close enough to walk — so was church — and car insurance premiums were outrageous. All of this was true, yet the real reason she had quit was because she was afraid. All the cars around her went too fast, they started honking at her, cursing her, rattling her to the point that she would make foolish mistakes like turning from the wrong lane. It was also important to have someplace to go. She had no one to see, all her friends were either gone or busy with their own family. What was the use in owning the car if she wasn't going to drive it? Owning it was enough, though. That sense of independence it gave her was something she wasn't ready to give up.

Sarah sat on the pink and blue bench in front of the mahogany dresser. The once-too-bright pink and blue stripes were now faded pastels. She used the pick to loosen her damp curls. It was when she looked in the mirror that she really felt old. Wrinkles creased her face like rivers on a map. A gray film covered the once-sparkling brown eyes. She looked at the brown and white photo resting on the dresser. The wedding couple was happy, although the groom looked uncomfortably stiff in his suit. His neck appeared to have been fused together with the collar of the shirt. He was tall, muscular and quite the looker. His black eyes and skin were excited and taut. She reached down and lightly touched the face of the man in the photo. "My, Hank, how you hated wearing suits, and you looking so fine in them." The bride was smiling, not at the camera but at him, feeling the desire and passion for the man and life they were about to share. The years had gone quickly, too quickly. For an instant she smelled his aftershave and heard his laughter. She paused for awhile, remembering and then shaking herself. "Woman, you better get yourself going now."

The snow on the sidewalk was over Sarah's knees. She shoveled a little at a time to keep from straining her back. The only other sound was young Ted Sullivan's snowblower across the street. He was one of the few whites left in the neighborhood. He was always checking on Sarah, making sure she was all right. He left the snowblower running and headed towards her, waving as he crossed the street.

"Snow is really something, isn't it, Sarah?" His breath was clearly visible as he spoke.

"It's sure more than something, a whole lot of people's Christmas plans will be changed. Oh, well, nothing can be done but shovel snow for now."

"Now Sarah, you know you shouldn't be shoveling this stuff." His voice and expression were as if he was scolding a child. "You just leave it. I'll do it as soon as I'm finished with mine."

"That's nice of you, Ted, but really, I can manage it. Besides, you'll be late for work."

"Nonsense, who won't be? I'll be over in a few minutes."

She smiled at him and lowered her voice. "What you won't do to impress an old black woman!" She knew there was no way those kids were going to make it out of town for Christmas, especially with a newborn. "Tell you what, Ted, you really want to impress this here woman and make her happy? You and that family come over here for Christmas!"

"We can't do that Sarah, impose on you and family like that."

"What family? Be jus' me and Old Tom Turkey if you don't come. Got all the fixin's, just need the appetites. Come at four o'clock.

He smiled at her, knowing his argument was lost.

"All right, Sarah. Lynn made some pies. We'll bring them."

"Fine. Don't have to worry about dessert, now, do I?"

"Thanks, Sarah."

"No need in thankin' me. You'll be doing me the favor."

"Well, thanks anyway." He laughed and headed back across the street.

"Give my best to Lynn and the baby — and thanks, Ted." He waved without looking back. he reminded her of another young man who had been considerate of her. Maybe that's why she liked Ted so much.

She was being helped down the steps by

her son, dressed in his Army uniform. He was smiling. My, how he spoiled her. Again she shook herself from her daydreaming. She grabbed her purse from the porch and started her walk to work. As she walked, the sound of Ted's snowblower could no longer be heard. She crossed University Avenue. The usually busy street was still. She turned on to State Street. As she looked up State Street, she gasped. The coldness of the air made her cough. It echoed down the deserted street. The beauty of the scene made her feel seven years old again. The houses, like the people in them were in a winter sleep. There was a beauty in the whiteness. Not a spot of brown or a blade of green could be seen. The worn old houses and construction sites had all turned into white ice castles. It wasn't just that the snow had covered everything, lined the veins of the bark on the trees, the street lights and eaves of the house, it was the snow itself. It was as if each flake was laid upon the other to capture and reflect what light it could. They appeared to be flakes of soft crystal. The clouds drifted low so that the tops of houses and trees disappeared into them. Sarah could see her mother in her long grey wool coat and burgundy hat and gloves. She was holding Sarah's hand, looking down at her smiling, "Baby, this only happens when heaven comes close to earth, touching it, and leaves behind whiteness and wonder...to remind us it is close by."

It was as if she was seeing the morning, feeling it with a seven year-old's heart. She was filled with wonder and a belief in the magic that touched her. She believed her mother, heaven was close by today. She felt it.

# Chapter Two

In the center of Dinkytown stands the First Methodist Church. The large blue-gray stones edged with snow, the violet clouds masking the tall bell tower gave the structure the appearance of a scene from medieval England.

The church tower was Nathan's home. He could appreciate the scene of white like no other. He didn't worry about the roads being plowed, the shoveling of sidewalks or the cold; not that he cared that much about such things when he was alive. Dinkytown was a playground for him, a lonely playground. He watched the first shop workers attempt to clear their sidewalks for business. Mrs. Murdock, the owner of Loving Laces stopped and straightened her back from the shoveling. He noticed the hair hanging down from the white wool cap had touches of gray. Had it been that long since he watched her grand opening? Nathan had developed a crush on her the day he saw her. She could have — still could — model any of the lingerie in her shop and guarantee a sale. Not that she ever did. Nathan had watched to make sure of it. He envied the gray in her hair and the fact that she was aging. He felt sad because he would eventually lose her, as he had others. He knew that being a ghost was being an invisible Peter Pan.

The wooden steps of the tower were frosted. He glided to the turn in the stairway and stopped. At the bottom of the steps, the snow had drifted in; gigantic icicles hung from the wooden rafters. The large spears of crystal reached downward into the drifts. They formed a small cell of ice and snow. Funnels of reflected light beamed into the center, forming a shining axis. It was a wheel of light, each beam a spoke. Speckles of snow and ice appeared to float in the air, shining like stars. Blues, greens and yellows twinkled about. Nathan started to pass through the mirage and suddenly he was trapped. He could no longer move forward or back. He was surrounded by a rainbow of light, suspending in it. A feeling of fear and thrill came over him.

As he waited to see what would happen next, a voice came, a soft soothing voice. "Nathan, this is your last Christmas. Make the most of it. You've wandered enough these years."

Nathan felt only fear now. He wondered who, what was happening to him. "What is this," he thought.

As if he had spoken the words, the voice replied: "Nathan, you know who I am. I have missed you."

Nathan felt a sense of panic. "If you missed me, why not show yourself to me?"

"I have enjoyed watching you play in that world. There are things for you and others that are unsettled; things you need to take care of. There will be help. . ."

"What things? Who?"

"Haven't you grown tired, Nathan?" The voice grew softer and disappeared.

"Of what?" Nathan realized he was not going to get an answer. The light had disappeared and he could move again. But he had known what the voice had meant — tired of being a ghost. He had enjoyed his unique status at first. He could play tricks, watch people do things they only did when they thought they were alone. He never was thirsty, hungry or tired. It was when he started noticing people enjoying the things he never had or never would have that he began to tire, saddened by being what he was. The laughter of friends together, the touch of lovers, the caring by someone when you're hurt or sad. He envied the struggle all of the living enjoyed.

There was comfort at the lack of footprints as he walked in the snow; it confirmed his ghostly status. He wasn't supposed to hear voices or see apparitions, he was supposed to cause them. "Ah, behave yourself, ghosts aren't supposed to worry!" That, he thought, was reason enough for Nathan to worry. He needed to see familiar sights and people.

His first stop was Tweed's florist shop. He went unnoticed to the rear of the shop to the refrigerator full of flowers. He took a single rose. Passing through the rear window, he emerged in the alley. Anyone in the alley would have been amazed to see a single rose floating in mid-air. He made his way to the rear of Mrs. Murdock's shop. He peeked around the corner to make sure she wasn't facing him. It wouldn't do to have her see a floating rose come to her door. He was in luck, she was shoveling with her back to him.

## Nathan's Christmas

He placed the rose at the doorstep and
waited. Mrs. Murdock took a shovelful of
snow and tossed it to the curb. It was then
she caught sight of the rose. She walked
over, kneeling down she picked up the rose
and brought it to her lips. She looked around
for any sign of who brought it; there never
was. She clasped the rose to her chest,
opened the door and went into her shop. As
he did every day, Nathan smiled at the expression on her face and left.

# Chapter Three

Robby opened the door to his apartment. The aroma of greasy food, stale beer and cigarettes flooded his nostrils. He promised himself he would wake early and get the place cleaned up. It was the eighth day in a row he had made that promise. He rubbed his temples, trying to squeeze out the three accidents, six DWIs and a stabbing. He was tired. He felt constantly tired and he just couldn't get himself recharged. He tossed his belt, holster and gun on the couch. His jacket didn't quite make it. He removed his badge and name tag, letting them drop to the coffee table. He removed his shirt, tossing it to the laundry corner. The apartment was quiet. It was what bothered him most, coming home to nothing.

He sat at the table, slicing cheese and salami for his breakfast, tossing the used knife in the sink. He slid open the glass patio door and reached for the snow-covered case of beer. The can was cold; popping the top he brought the can to his lips. The beer sprayed his face and T-shirt. "Nuts! " He quickly wiped the beer away.

He ate the cheese and meat without tasting it, forcing it down with swallows of beer. He stared at the letter lying before him on the table. He had read the letter over and over. It was from his ex-wife's attorney. Among all the legal jargon was the fact that she wanted Robby to give up all legal rights to his son Jeff, so her new husband could adopt him. In return for giving Jeff up, Robby would be relieved of support payments and debts from the marriage and reimbursed for past payments of ten thousand dollars. The letter smelled of his ex-father-in-law. It brought to mind the sense of bribery and that money was the answer to everything. He remembered how his father-in-law had lashed out with disdain and anger when his daughter married a "cop." Robby sighed as he pushed the letter away. He felt an ache in his chest and the feeling of tears starting to form. It made him feel cheap, insignificant.

He had become an interruption in his son's life. He could only afford to see him once a year since they moved back East. He and Jeff had become strangers pretending to be father and son. He could feel his stomach sour and his chest tighten at the thought of his son's last visit. Robby knew Jeff meant no hurt. Robby had even brought the subject up, but listening to the litany of the things Jeff and his stepfather were doing together brought more pain than he thought possible.

## Nathan's Christmas

The stories of deep sea fishing, camping, horseback riding, the concerts and plays brought the realization of how cheated he had been from the divorce and how distant he had become from his son. Robby took the beer and dumped it in the sink. He had lost Jeff and someone else was raising him, sharing with him, teaching him values. What kind of values could Robby teach his son if he signed away his rights? He hoped just being there someday would be enough for his son. Maybe he was fooling himself. Maybe it was his way of striking back at his father-in-law or just financial foolishness. He grabbed the letter, crumpled it and tossed it into the garbage. "You can stick it, all of you!"

Robby pulled the clothes off his bed and set his alarm for noon. Today he knew that he would clean the apartment; anger was a great motivator. He lifted the shade and looked out; the snow was untouched. He imagined the times he and Jeff went sledding

together, the snowball fights and fort building, the giggles, smell of wet clothes, sting-
ing fingers and pink cheeks and the hot
chocolate. Now, his life was in reverse of everyone else's. He was going to bed, they
were getting up. When he had breakfast,
they were having dinner. When he was off,
they were working. It was the loneliness, not
having someone to listen to, talk with. . . At
twenty eight, he felt old.

# Chapter Four

Nathan was standing in the aisle when Brian and Jim unlocked the door to their music store, Off The Wall. He knew they would be having the same argument. Jim, the oldest, was heavyset with a Groucho mustache that made him look like a walrus without the tusks. Brian was taller and thinner, quite handsome in a feminine way.

Jim shook his head. "I'm not listening to that album one more time."

"Jim, you know what happens when. . ."

"I don't know anything except a kid took all our albums and switched them all around. Besides, I've told you to watch those brats."

Brian smiled. "It wasn't any kid or kids. You know it happened after the store closed."

"How do I know it wasn't you? You're always doing things to drive me crazy. Like now!"

"Will you explain how that album is on the turntable every morning...even the nights I don't work? Huh, tell me that!"

Jim closed one eye and stared at his brother with the other. "Like I said, you yutz, you're trying to drive me nuts."

"Don't give me that, you know darn well what. . ."

"I don't want to hear it. Don't give me that spirit stuff, a ghost that wants to wake up to Carol King every morning."

"You have a better explanation? Want to tempt fate once more, and spend a week recategorizing all the albums? Not me. It hasn't happened since we played it, has it?"

Jim walked over to the turntable. Sure enough, under the smoke colored plastic cover was the "Tapestry" album ready to be played. "Hmpf—well, at least I don't have to listen to it this time. I'm going out and shovel." He grabbed the shovel from the closet and headed down the aisle like a bear awakened from his winter sleep. He passed right through Nathan.

Brian switched on the turntable and the speakers that lined all four walls. "I wonder what he or she looks like; how old, if there is a way we could see..."

Jim stopped at the door. "What are you mumbling about?"

"The ghost. Who is it, I wonder?"

Jim rolled his eyes. "If you keep talking that way, you'll find out soon enough, because you'll be one!"

Nathan laughed and got himself comfortable on the counter as the song "I Feel the Earth Move" reverberated through the store.

## Chapter Five

C hris slipped out of bed. He took off his pajamas and slipped into the worn jeans and cotton shirt he had laid out for himself the night before. On went his socks and sneakers, his movements picking up speed as he dressed. He grabbed his pajamas. The narrow hallway to his mother's bedroom was strewn with her clothes. The trail of clothes identified the order she had undressed; jacket, skirt, blouse, slip, bra, panties and shoes.

## Nathan's Christmas

He turned the knob slowly as not to make any noise. He pushed the door just enough to reveal his mother's bed. He hoped the trail of clothes was a sign that she was alone. His mother was sprawled on the top of the bed looking more unconscious than asleep. He studied her face. He saw the pretty girl behind the alcohol-swollen and sagging skin. The past evening's make-up streaked her face. He felt a sadness that choked him. How pretty she had been, and might be still if only. . .he didn't allow himself to finish the thought. He had things to do.

He turned the radio on in the kitchen. Chris knew there would be no school today because of the snow, but wanted the satisfaction of hearing it officially. He washed the dishes from supper and his cereal bowl from the morning. Then, like a bee from flower to flower, he went from table to table, gathering filled ashtrays, empty glasses, and stale beer cans. He wiped the tables clean and returned with a new load of dishes to be done.

The gallon of wine sitting on the counter had been left open. He screwed the cap on. He slid the stool over to the pantry. The bottle was heavy and he strained to lift it over his head, putting it on the top shelf. The price of hiding it was too great; the sting of his mother's slaps wasn't worth it. Putting it there was at least a delaying action to her drinking and he measured that in minutes. She wouldn't be awake for another three hours. Then, she would stagger to the kitchen table, drink coffee and smoke cigarettes until she had enough energy to turn on the television. The coffee! He hadn't made the coffee yet. He hurried to get the coffee started. This would insure that he would beat Mrs. Billings to the laundry machines. If not, she would tie the machines up for the entire day. No matter how large she was, how one person had so much laundry was beyond him. He imagined Mrs. Billings going from apartment to apartment asking if they needed anything washed; every apartment that is, except his mother's. Mrs. Billings disliked his mother a lot, a feeling that was mutual. Mrs. Billings was nice to Chris when he was alone, patting his head, offering cookies, clothes and such. It was the only time he felt poor, and for that he disliked her. It was hard enough for a kid to climb on top of the washers to insert coins, guessing how much soap to use, how to separate the clothes. They had nothing white in their wardrobes any more; everything was shades of pastel pinks and blues.

The washers swished as Chris made his way up the stairs. He heard the door to Mrs. Billing's apartment open and he ducked out the back door of the apartments to avoid her. He felt foolish hiding from her. He just didn't want to deal with her looks and any snide comments about his mother. In the distance sounds of spinning tires stuck in the snow could be heard. The air smelled clean, the snow was well over his knees. The tree branches looked like crystal flames.

Across the open fields, and past the 7-Eleven, stood Fullerton's Toy Store. Surrounded by the amber lamps and covered in snow, the structure appeared an orange Oz. It was a magic place. Chris spent hours there pretending every toy was his. He had very few toys of his own, yet he didn't feel cheated. He knew someday it would change. Life would turn out well for him. Until then, the snow would have to do. The forts, snowmen and snowball fights. He opened the door, and ran up the stairs. He had to ready himself for the battle.

# Chapter Six

Bridgeman's Ice Cream and Cafe was one of Nathan's favorite places. It preserved the old time atmosphere of people sharing a malt or burger together, not being herded through like the fast food places, a number without a choice. The large front windows were partially frosted and the white front disappeared into the snow. He walked up to the window and looked in. Sarah was behind the counter. Nathan smiled to himself as he watched her work.

*Nathan's Christmas*

She was one of Nathan's favorite people. No
matter how rushed she was or how badly
things went, she always had a smile for those
around. She even withstood his pranks of
changing the silverware around, putting all
the forks together, the knives and so on,
making food items change places or holding
the cash register shut. Even when he was
alive, he teased only those he really cared
about. With the others he was only polite.
But he made everyone else do Sarah justice.
He made sure customers tipped her well.
Sometimes he took an extra five from a billfold and left it on the counter. Any money he
found around the street he would leave on
the counter for her and he did nasty things to
any customer that gave her a bad time.

She was alone now. He watched as she replaced the full coffee pot with an empty one
and started the brewer. She turned and
looked right at him. Her brown eyes grew
large. She appeared to see him. He stepped
back in reaction to her stare. She pointed at

him and motioned him to come in. Nathan looked around thinking she was waving to someone else. Surely she wasn't motioning to him. There was no one else there. Sarah continued to wave in a frantic matter. He pointed to himself and watched her nod approvingly. He felt a shudder of cold run through him. His breath was like smoke in the air. But he wasn't supposed to have a breath. He wasn't supposed to feel cold either, but he did. He felt weak. He also felt pulled to Sarah, to actually be able to talk with her. He walked to the door and started to step through it. Let Sarah see this! Bang! Pain circled his eyes and nose. As he hit the door, he actually felt it. It was not painful like when he was alive. It was more a sensation of aching throbs. He looked down at the door knob, reaching for it he felt a strange sensation. Cold. It was cold and he was cold. He walked in and a little bell rang from atop the door announcing his entrance. He was confused. He was human.

## Nathan's Christmas

"My lord, son, look at you! It's below zero and you're dressed like you're in California. I know your mom taught you better. You're white as a ghost." Sarah ended her scolding with a smile. The boy reminded her of a puppy found on a doorstep. "Now, you sit right down here and I'll get you some coffee to warm them bones of yours."

Nathan sat at the counter. He was numb, but not from the cold. He looked down at himself. He stared at his hand as he opened and closed it. He found it hard to get used to the feeling of a body, muscles moving, joints bending and eyes blinking. He was wearing loafers, now filled with snow, faded jeans and a blue flannel shirt. When he thought of it, these were the clothes he had been wearing when he was killed. He quickly inspected himself and a sigh of relief escaped when he found no blood stains. Someone or something had restored his clothes to the way they were before the accident. He remembered the words, "make the most of it, share your gifts." What gifts? If he had been alive, this would be called a nightmare, but what do spirits have? Sarah watched him flex his hand and inspect himself. At first she thought maybe he was on drugs, but something told her that wasn't the case. He acted more like he was lost. She brought the coffee and set it in front of him. "Now drink this and see if we can get some color back into those cheeks."

The warmth of the cup felt like ecstasy to his hands. He brought the cup to his mouth and took a large swallow. The hot liquid scalded his mouth. He spit it out. Coffee sprayed across the counter.

Drops of coffee hit Sarah. She grabbed a rag and started to wipe off the counter. "Now I know I make a mean cup of coffee, but most of my customers sip it. Hot is hot."

"Sorry, Sarah." Nathan was surprised by the sound of his voice. He saw Sarah stop in mid-wipe and her eyes searched his.

"How do you know my name? You

haven't been here before, I'd remember you."

"Just heard the other kids mention you. How Sarah at Bridgeman's is always smiling and treats you good." He felt his cheeks flush, the answer even sounded flimsy to him.

"Right. Like I'm supposed to believe that. Never mind. So you know my name. You want some breakfast, or is spittin' coffee enough for you this morning?"

Suddenly he felt hungry. "Sure. Eggs, bacon, toast and orange juice."

"How you want the eggs?"

"Over easy." He watched Sarah as she went into the kitchen. He glanced down the counter at all the neat place settings. Without thinking, he went to the last setting and started gathering all of the forks. He started changing them so that each place setting had all the same pieces of silverware. When he reached the third setting he looked up. Sarah was watching him with one eyebrow raised and her arms crossed in front of her.

He smiled. "Habit, I guess." It was difficult to remember he wasn't invisible anymore.

"Uh huh." Sarah remembered all the times she had turned around at work to find the silverware arranged in just that way. Most of the time she had been alone. She had blamed it on poltergeist or senility; preferring the first explanation. She was sure the boy hadn't been here before, yet there was something familiar, comfortable about his presence. "You're a little strange, even for a white boy. You live around here?"

"Near the church." He started putting the silverware back. "I've been away for quite awhile."

A bell rang. Sarah went to the kitchen, returning with his breakfast. The smell was overpowering, the scent was awesome to him. The sharp taste of bacon was a delight. He remembered how this was his favorite meal. He realized this must be what it was like when he was a child tasting these things

45

for the first time. Before he realized it, the food was gone. A wave of contentment settled over him. He sipped the coffee, the bitterness awakening his taste buds. He had no thought of moving until Sarah ripped the check off the pad, placing it in front of him. She smiled. "More coffee anytime you're ready."

Nathan shook his head. Panic started to set in. Money! You need to pay for it, you idiot. He couldn't stiff Sarah. He checked the rear pocket of his jeans. No billfold. Then his left front pocket. Nothing. He sighed as his right hand felt the crisp feeling of bills and the cold touch of coins. He left a dollar tip and went to the register and gave her the exact change. Sarah stared down at the money.

"Is there something wrong?"

"You rob a coin collection or what? I haven't seen stuff like this forever. Quarters without copper, silver certificate dollars and an Indianhead nickel that looks brand new.

You sure you want to give these to me?"

"It's all I have. Just keep anything you make from them. Really, I don't care."

He didn't wait for a reply. Outside, he stopped at the window. Sarah was watching him, then waved for him to wait. She ran into the kitchen and returned carrying something. She ran out to him and handed him a leather jacket lined with gold satin.

"You take this, to keep you warm, hear? Some high roller left it here. As drunk as he was, he'll never remember where he left it." She reached into her pocket pulling out two bright purple and white checked mittens. "They don't exactly match but they'll keep you warm."

"I can't take these, Sarah."

"You can and will. No arguments. My word, if my son. . ." For an instant she recognized the feeling she had for him. It hurt and felt good at the same time. She gave him a hug and felt him return it. She forced herself to release him.

_Nathan's Christmas_

"You take care of yourself."

"Thanks, Sarah, you're really something..."

Yeah, and you're crazy..."

"Guess I am." He watched as Sarah headed back. "Merry Christmas, Sarah."

"Merry Christmas, Nathan." She wondered how she knew his name. She scratched her head and continued back to the restaurant. She turned to wave and he was gone. No tracks; nothing. Just gone.

# Chapter Seven

Megan slammed the phone down hard. She was letting her anger get away. She even felt a little foolish. She had started by pretending to be angry because the airport was closed and she wouldn't be able to spend the holidays with her dad. What she really felt was relief, but the pretending got out of hand and became real. This had been happening to her since she was small. She let out a sigh. At least the guilt wouldn't be on her because she chose to spend the holidays with her dad and stepmother instead of her mom. Who was she kidding? She knew her mother. The fact that she didn't make it to her dad's didn't matter. It was the intent that counted. It had been this way since she was six and her parents divorced. She just wished they would let her love them and not make it some sort of competition.

She lifted the receiver. She listened to the dial tone and then replaced the handset. She could wait to call her dad. She lay down on the loveseat, staring up at the ceiling. What was happening to her? She was having a hard time making decisions. She wasn't enjoying school and her personal life was zip. She reached over and picked up her grade sheet from the University. Two C's, two D's and an "Incomplete" that would be an F in the near future. She knew she wasn't dumb. She just didn't do the work. It all seemed so plastic to her. The professors threw out bits of so-called knowledge. They didn't care about anything except doing their research and getting published. She saw her fellow students as frivolous, not caring about real issues. She knew life wasn't all seriousness, but there was more to it than drunken frat parties. What was it that would make her happy? She felt the tears roll from the corner of her eyes. She couldn't answer the question. She could feel strings tugging at her stomach. Her lips quivered and a dark fog of failure passed through her mind. She felt so tired — tired of putting on acts for everyone, tired of not "knowing" and just plain tired. She knew being with her dad would make her feel even more like a failure. He never criticized. He was always supportive, as was her stepmother. They just wanted her happy. Their only mistake was that they defined happiness on their terms, not hers. The disappointment was hers. She wanted so much to be a success for them and had sacrificed her values for theirs.

She looked over at the little artificial tree with the small lights twinkling. The wrapped presents engulfed the tree. Three were wrapped in expensive green and red stripes with gold ribbon, two were rectangular and one was a jewelry-size box. She walked over and picked up the small box and flipped the card open. "Paul, with love, for the time and moments shared. Merry Christmas. Love, Megan." Her fingers caressed the box, turning it and turning it, her eyes clouding as her mind focused on an evening two weeks ago. Paul had been standing close to her, his hands stuffed in his jeans pockets, the collar of the varsity jacket pulled up to protect his neck. He swayed from foot to foot. His words were soft.

"I'm sorry, Megan. I won't be spending Christmas with you. The truth is, there is someone else. It just happened. Well, it's best you and I don't see each other again."

Paul had walked away without Megan saying a word. It wasn't that there weren't things she wanted to say or ask. She just couldn't get the air into her lungs to speak.

She hadn't heard from or spoken to him since. The loss of trust left only silence.

She put the present back and walked to her frost-covered windows. She scraped a small opening and looked down into the street. Her first thought was what a pain it was going to be to shovel her car out. Then she noticed how wondrously white everything was. There was something out there for her. She brought her fingers to the windows, letting them melt the ice. The cold felt good. She leaned her head against the window. Christmas alone. Maybe it was better that way. The snow looked so enticing. Like a child she wanted to play in it, eat it, maybe even build a snowman. But first the car. She didn't like feeling stranded. Besides, it was something to do. Keeping busy was best.

People came out into the snow like the Munchkins came out to greet Dorothy. Slowly they came — shoveling and brushing doors, windows and roofs clean. Then the children started to play — laughing. Snowmen became alive and snowballs filled the air. There was gaiety that only comes with cheating a school day.

Nathan walked around and through people, making sure that he was once again a ghost. He passed through doors and cars. The incident with Sarah had shaken him. He decided to return to Off the Wall. Music would help him think.

Jim was at the counter putting labels on the newly arrived albums. Bobby McFadden was singing "My Garden" on the stereo. Nathan could not see Brian. He passed by Jim and went into the stereo room. He took "his" album down, flipping to side two. He lifted the needle, replaced the record and set the needle back down. Carol King's voice immediately made Nathan feel better.

He heard Jim's voice yelling, "All right, enough is enough! I'm going to kick your sweet butt! You're driving me nuts with. . ." Jim's voice ceased when he entered the room.

He had expected to find Brian there, playing a trick on him. The room was empty. He started toward the turntable reaching to stop the music. Instead, he stopped. Turning, he left the room, again yelling, "Brian, where are you? This isn't funny. You dork, this isn't funny."

Nathan went to the counter where Jim had been working. He quickly removed all the labels on the albums. He stuck the labels on the counter so that they spelled "HI". He watched as Jim approached. Jim was mumbling to himself about what he was going to do to Brian and cursing the music. He reached for the label stickers. He stared at the new albums; all the labels were gone. He glanced around, trying to change his slight fear into anger. Then he noticed the greeting on the counter. He slapped his hand to his face in frustration. He heard the door open and looked up to see Jim come in carrying a white bag. He watched Jim hesitate as he recognized the music.

Jim yelled, "Where were you?"

"I went to get us bagels and coffee, what's. . ."

"Right! Well, you better cut this stuff out!"

"I didn't. . ."

"And you better not do it again!"

Brian walked over to the counter and set the bag down. He noticed the letters spelled out. "Cute, Jim. Cute."

"You did it. Don't tell me that you didn't. I don't want to hear it."

"Sure, Jim. I hear you're playing your favorite album again, too. . ."

"If I hear one word from you about ghosts, I'll smack you in the mouth."

Brian started to laugh. "Right. That's the spirit, Jim. There isn't a ghost of a chance that I would mention it." He laughed as Jim continued to mumble threats.

Nathan left the brothers arguing. They were closest when they argued. Neither was married, but they had each other. Over the years Nathan had come to realize that was enough for them. He started walking toward the campus. He felt good after leaving the music shop.

He was walking with his head down, staring at the snow when he heard a voice call out, "Pardon me. Could you help me? I'm stuck — I mean my car is stuck."

Nathan looked up and the young lady appeared to be directing her conversation to him. He glanced around and found himself alone. She was talking to him. "I guess I could. Sure." He walked toward her. She was wearing one of those floppy stocking hats. Her dark brown hair stuck out of the edges. She had a small curved nose, a beautiful cream complexion and green eyes. Irish green, Nathan thought. She was petite and very pretty.

"I'm Megan. I really don't know why I want the car out anyway. Maybe independence, I don't know. I was going out to the airport. No flights scheduled, but maybe I could find out my options. Supposed to go home for the holidays, though it doesn't look like it now. What's your name?"

"Nathan." He felt warm just listening to how easily she opened up to a complete stranger. Her speech was quick, the words were like bullets. He looked at the red Mustang. She had shoveled around the car, but more shoveling was needed in front, behind and underneath. "I hope you're not in a hurry. This may take a while. Where's the shovel?"

"I have it over here. I really appreciate this, Nathan." She looked at him and felt a trusting attachment to him. His eyes were surrounded by mischief, his dark blonde hair flowed to the whim of the wind. His whole face changed when he smiled. Otherwise, he had a sad look to him. He reminded her of a lost boy that she had once helped. "Home for the holidays?"

"What?" The snow was giving way easily for him.

"Are you home for the holidays?"

"Not really. Live near the church." He noticed that the exercise didn't tire him and his muscles didn't ache. He dug out the rear tires, then the front and got the snow that had drifted under the car. Megan followed as he went.

"You have family here?"

"No. My parents are dead. No brothers or sisters. I'm it."

Megan frowned. "I'm sorry." Great move, Megan, she thought.

"It's OK. It was a long time ago. Get in, start her up and we'll see if we can rock it out."

The car whined as she shifted from forward to reverse and back to forward without letting up on the gas. Nathan went to the rear of the car and pushed it as it rocked forward. He didn't push hard, but the car moved beneath his effort with ease. It moved so easily that he fell forward. He caught his hand on the bumper and his face slammed into the trunk. He pulled his hand back expecting it to be bleeding; he had felt his palm slide across the sharp edge of metal. There was no mark. He glanced in the window to see his reflection. He thought at least his nose would be bleeding. It wasn't. Why should it be, he thought. You need a heartbeat and pulse to bleed.

Megan stopped as soon as she heard the "thunk" of Nathan hitting the car. "You all right?" She jumped out of the car, kneeled beside Nathan and helped him up, brushing off the snow.

"I'm fine. It was my own fault. I think I can make it from here." He stood up. "Hope you can get home. Merry Christmas." He started to walk away.

Something tugged inside her. She didn't want to see him go, not like this anyway. "This may sound crazy. It does a little even to me. But since we're both going to be alone, I was wondering if you would like to join me for a Christmas Eve dinner?"

At that moment Nathan had he never felt more alive and confused. "I don't think. . ."

"I'm sorry. Of course you have other plans. I. . ."

"No, no other plans. I would love to. I just don't know if I will be. . ."

"Good, it's settled. Let's say around seven." She went to her car and returned handing him a piece of paper. She lightly kissed his cheek. "My, you'd better get in, you're really cold. Now you have my address and phone number. And thanks for the help."

He watched her drive away and when she turned the corner he realized his breath had gone with her. He was a ghost again. He wondered what would happen if he tried. Well, he would just have to find out.

Nathan wandered aimlessly. He glided through buildings and parks and ended up by the river unnoticed. He wanted to figure out what was happening to him. He thought through the encounters with Sarah and

## Nathan's Christmas

Megan.  On each occasion he was alone with the person.  This was strange considering that the meetings happened in a restaurant and on a main street.  You would think someone would stop by for breakfast, coffee to go, or a car would pass by.  He looked at the river flowing black water.  What bothered him most was,  like the water,  he had no control of where he was going.  An invisible current was pulling him toward someplace or something.  Being a ghost wasn't all that great,  but he had gotten used to it.  It was the unknown that scared him — the unknown of where the current,  the voice, was taking him.

He decided to start at the beginning, where he died.  He had always avoided that street but he was in need of answers, no matter what painful memories he had to turn up.  There again,  he was thinking as if he were alive and having feelings,  something ghosts were not to be concerned about. He knew from that alone he was heading for something — something that was to happen in less than twenty four hours.

The orange from the street lamps formed circles of gold along University Avenue. There were a few cars making their way home. The banks of billowed snow stood over five feet high on each side of the street. A few flakes of snow hovered in the air. Nathan sat on the bank in front of the Natural History Museum. He watched a figure in a ski mask running on the other side of the road, either a jogger or a very slow robber. He chuckled. It had been summer when Nathan had last been at this spot and he had been alive. He and his cousins had planned a trip to the lake for some water skiing and he was running late as usual. The traffic had been heavy as he waited for the traffic light to change. He watched the light turn from yellow to red for the oncoming traffic and saw the walk signal light up. The driver of the Cadillac never even saw the light or knew that it was red. Nathan watched as the car slammed into him. Both legs broke as he headed toward the windshield. His head collapsed against it. He felt his insides tear up. The irony was that the only pain he felt was from the superficial scrapes from his slide on the pavement. He remembered hearing a whistle, seeing the policeman bending over him and then the people talking. He heard the policeman say: "My God, hang in there, son." Then Nathan remembered saying something, but what was it? Crying, the policeman had picked him up and held him. The last thing Nathan remembered was seeing his dad. But that was impossible because his dad had died from cancer two years earlier. His dad had been saying something to him. He had been smiling. Then there was darkness. He had to remember what it was. Somehow it seemed important.

Nathan was grabbed by the arm. He didn't know what startled him more, the fact that he hadn't seen the man approach or the fact that he felt it.

"You want to get yourself killed, son?" He recognized the voice immediately as that of Robby, the police officer. He turned slowly to Robby. Their eyes met. Nathan felt the grip tighten. Robby turned white and, for a moment, his legs gave way. He started to fall. Nathan grabbed him until he could regain his balance. "I'm sorry, son. You just looked so much like someone who. . ."

"It's all right, officer. I just have one of those faces that look like everyone else's."

"No, it isn't that. He was killed almost where you are standing. Maybe it was the thought of that. You sure look like him. But that has to be going on seven years ago. Still, let's get out of the street, shall we?"

Neither talked while they walked to the other side of the street. Nathan took a look around and, sure enough, there were no other people or cars on the road.

"You mentioned someone was killed here. Were you here when it happened?"

"Not exactly. I got here within minutes,

though. He was about your age. A drunk, I should say a guy with a few too many, didn't see the light and hit him. When I got here he was still alive, but not for long."

"Did he say anything before he died?"

Robby raised his eyebrow, brought his hand to his chin and stared a long time before answering. "Yes, he did. I was a rookie that year and it was the first time I had seen anyone die. You don't forget that sort of thing. He said, `Four left to go. Not yet. Four to go.' And then he smiled and mumbled something else. Then, he was gone."

"Four left to go, not yet, four to go?" Nathan wondered what he had meant. "Strange last words. You have any idea what he was saying?"

Robby shook his head.

"Since then, I've heard many last words and most meant nothing except to the one saying them." Robby looked at Nathan with the eye of a policeman. "You all right, son?

You look pretty pale."

Looking back at Robby, Nathan wondered who looked worse. He felt sorry that he had played tricks on him. There was strain in his face, strain from carrying some unresolved hurt. The lines around his mouth told Nathan that smiles didn't frequent his face very often.

"Yeah, I'm fine." He started to walk away and could feel Robby watching him. They walked together along the sidewalk. Nathan wanted to say something to him but he wasn't sure how. "You're a good cop, Robby."

"Sure."

"No, really. I've seen you around here. You really care about the people around here. You take time for kids and old people." He saw a smile begin to form and noticed Robby looked so much younger. "How come you're a cop?"

"Lately I've been asking myself the same question," He glanced around, making sure all was in order. "The law was something I thought I could count on. I've always needed that."

"I know what you mean. To have some-thing to hold on to. Something no one could take away."

"Yeah, and I wanted to make a differ-ence."

"You have."

"Maybe, but life is more than — Listen to me, running off this way. I'd better start serving the public I care so much about." Again, the years seemed to peel away with his smile.

Nathan turned and gave him a wave.

Headlight beams passed through Nathan as a car turned on to University Avenue and he knew he was a ghost again. He walked through the Commons, then fraternity row and past Ernie's Greek restaurant. He under-stood that his last words had to do with what was happening now but he didn't under-stand the connection. He crossed the bridge to the West Bank, listening to the clock strike ten. He even wished he could be tired. Then at least he would be something. He wanted to be away for awhile, go to a place where he didn't have to think. He thought of where he might want to go. Then he knew. Fullerton's Toy store. It was the largest toy store in the state, a place Nathan had visited many times to watch the kids overwhelmed by the variety of stuffed animals, dolls, trains and cars. Any child's wish could be answered at Fullerton's.

## Chapter Eight

The store was noisier than Nathan had remembered. People were crowding the aisles. With the storm, of course, many had been prevented from doing their Christmas shopping, and now there were less than thirty hours for buying. He watched one man swear because he couldn't find what he was looking for. A woman argued with another lady over who was going to get the last mechanical puppy. Children were saying over and over, "I want that, I want that."

## Nathan's Christmas

Nathan wondered how many really had the feeling and spirit of Christmas. Fullerton's had been more fun and full of charm when he had been there alone. There was a lack of joy about the place now. He could feel the weight of it. It saddened him and then, he realized he was feeling again.

The stuffed animal section was a little less crowded. He thought probably with video games and walking, talking and wetting babies there wasn't much call for something just to cuddle with. At the end of the aisle was a large swimming pool filled with all sizes and colors of stuffed animals. As if guarding these small creatures was a large stuffed dog. He had to be almost seven feet tall. He was light brown with a white chest. Each black ear was three feet long and drooped alongside his head. His nose was black, surrounded by white fur with brown freckles. He had gigantic brown eyes and legs like stove pipes with each paw detailed in black, white and brown. His large brown eyes, whiskers, smile and large tongue made him look like a big pup that wanted to please and be loved. There was something very real about the animal. Nathan expected that at any moment, the tail would start to wiggle.

From the left paw hung a large sign: "GUESS THE NUMBER OF STUFFED ANIMALS IN THE POOL AND WIN ME PLUS $1,500.00. LOVE, HERBIE." There was a large box next to the pool to place your guess and entry forms. "How many you think is in there, Mister?"

Nathan looked down. Alongside him was a boy. He was wearing faded blue corduroy pants that were white at the knees. He had a stained old gray parka with stuffing coming out of each of the elbows. He had white blonde hair and excited blue eyes. His head was slightly tilted as if in curious thought.

"I'm not sure, but there's over ten thousand in there, I bet. How many do you think there are?"

The boy was glad to be asked. A smile appeared. He looked at the pool of stuffed animals, "I bet there is twenty, maybe thirty thousand..." He scuffed his shoes on the ground, lowering his head. "Maybe I'm too old to have a stuffed dog, but Herbie sure looks like he needs a friend."

"Well, I don't know about too old, 'cause if I had a place for him, I sure would want him. Besides, we all need friends." Those words nagged at him. He pushed them back and looked down at the boy, who was smiling again. Even with the smile he looked old, older than his years.

"What's your name?"

"Chris. Chris Hamilton."

"Well hi, Chris. I'm Nathan. Should you be talking to strangers?"

"Guess not, but you're OK. I can tell." Chris was sure of what he said. He didn't know why. He just felt it.

"Have your parents made your guess for you?"

"I don't have a dad and Mom's not here.

She's — she's too busy right now." The habit to protect his mom was too strong for him to tell the truth that she was at a bar drinking and would be there until it closed. He felt bad that he had to lie.

"I've got an idea. You go looking around the rest of the store, let's say for about twenty minutes, then come back here and I'll have the number to win Herbie. What do you say?"

"Sure. You're going to count them all?" He studied Nathan for a long time. "This isn't a joke, is it, Nathan?"

"No joke, I promise." Chris walked away, constantly turning to check on Nathan. He reached another aisle, turned and was gone.

Soon an announcement blared over the store's P.A. system, "Mr. Cooper, aisle six please." The shoppers continued looking for their special gifts, not realizing the store manager and security had been summoned to aisle six. Barton, the store manager, walked fast without trying to draw attention to himself. He could see Dexter, the security director at the end of the aisle. Dexter was standing there wide-eyed, his mouth gaping. He looked as if he were catching flies with his tongue. "All right, Dexter, what is it?" Barton noticed that Dexter's feet were surrounded by stuffed animals — bears, frogs, bunnies and puppies in pink, blue, yellow and green. "Dexter, did you hear me? What in the world is going on?"

Dexter did not answer, he just raised his arm and pointed toward the pool. There in the center of the pool were bears and puppies flying in the air. Some would fly up and then just stop as if defying gravity, then fly to the side of the pool. "What do you think it is?"

The stuffed animals continued their flights as Barton tried to see who in the pool was throwing them. "I can't see anyone, but you get in there and get the kid out."

Dexter moved to the pool. He put his foot over the side as if he expected to feel ice cold water. Smack! A teddy bear hit him square between the eyes. As Dexter tried to recover his balance, a second, third and fourth stuffed animal pummeled his head and shoulders. He fell to the floor. He looked up to see a red-faced Barton staring down at him.

"What are you doing, Dexter? Now you get up and get that kid out of there! You're head of security for crying out loud, and you're letting teddy bears get the best of you!"

Dexter could feel his face flush as he rose. He glanced around seeing people starting to gather by the pool. Great, he thought, just what he needed was an audience. He clenched his teeth; protecting his eyes with his arm, he slid over the side of the pool. teddies and puppies came soaring at him. He was waist deep in animals and losing his balance. He could see no source for the fly-ing animals. He reached in with his arm, try-ing to feel an arm or leg to grab. Nothing! He stood there looking. He took a step when all of a sudden his other foot was pulled forward. He fell like a cut tree. As his face slammed into a giraffe staring up at him, he realized someone had tied his shoelaces together.

Laughter was growing when Dexter's head peeked out of the stuffed animals. He slipped his shoes off and tossed them out of the pool. He stood up as the last teddy landed. The pool was silent. He could feel the hair on his neck stand up. It was foolish to be afraid, but afraid he was. He imagined something nibbling on his feet or grabbing his legs. He waded back and forth; seeing and feeling nothing but animals. He turned to Barton and shrugged his shoulders. "Nothing."

"Well, keep looking. No one's come out. And try staying on your feet this time."

Nathan slipped unnoticed through the crowd that had gathered. The crowd stood around the silent pool for fifteen minutes before they started to disperse. He found Chris sitting next to the rack of bikes. His head was in his hands. There were drops on the floor from tears. "Chris?"

The boy looked up and a grin appeared that could light up a room. "I tried to get to the pool but the crowd was so big. I thought someone had won Herbie. Then I thought I was too late, that you had left."

"I'm here, but we've got a small problem." He saw the smile fade. "No. No, I have the number for you, actually two numbers."

"Two numbers?"

"In all those stuffed animals there was a kangaroo, and in her pouch was a baby kangaroo. So, does that count as one or two stuffed animals? If you count it as one, your guess is 12,344, and if they count as two, your number is 12,345."

"Which guess do I make? There's only one guess per person."

"You could put a guess in for yourself, and one for your mom."

Chris was silent for a long time and then shook his head no. "If Mom wins that money it would kill her. She would drink herself to death. No, maybe I should just..." He frowned. He realized he had betrayed his mother by disclosing their secret, yet Nathan's expression hadn't changed. He smiled. Nathan could be trusted.

"Wait, listen. Just go to the manager and ask him. Does it count as one or two? Then you'll know what your guess is to be."

The boy laughed and smiled. "That's fair. Otherwise it's like they're trying to trick us or something." His smile disappeared again, he squinted his eyes and stuck his hands in his pockets. "This isn't cheating is it? We aren't doing something wrong or illegal?"

Nathan couldn't keep from laughing. If he were alive, it sure would be illegal, a felony at that. But he imagined that as a ghost he had some slack on such matters, especially since Man's law really didn't apply to him.

"Nah, this isn't cheating. I told you I would have a number for you and I do. There's no way they would let me in there and count them, now is there? Besides, how do you know that I'm giving you the right number?"

Chris tilted his head at him and the smile reappeared. "I don't know how, Nathan, but this is the exact number, and I want to thank you for it."

"I figure Herbie couldn't have a better friend."

"I've really got to go, Nathan. Mom may need me. Thanks again."

"You bet." He watched as Chris headed to the manager's office. He stopped, turned around and ran back to Nathan. He hugged and squeezed him. At that moment Nathan envied Herbie.

"Merry Christmas, Nathan."

"Merry Christmas, Chris." A single tear trickled down Nathan's cheek.

# Chapter Nine

Four to go. He drifted about thinking time was becoming short. He knew that certain people could see him, and that he was only seen when they were alone. Something that Chris said about friends reached something long forgotten. Then it hit him. Could he be seen by them again? He headed for Bridgeman's and hoped Sarah would be there.

He was pleasantly surprised when he saw Sarah cleaning the counter. Normally, she would have gone home long ago. He also was pleased when his hand made contact with the door knob.

Sarah greeted him with a smile. "You still out and about?"

"I have some last-minute things to take care of."

"Well, son, I'll offer you some coffee if you promise not to go spittin' it all over the place."

He laughed. He felt warm just being around her. "You got a deal, Sarah. You wouldn't want to join me, would you?

"I don't see why not. Only had three customers all evening." Sarah's large hips waddled as she walked. She got two cups of coffee and took them to the booth by the window. Flakes of snow started to drift down gently. They were large flakes, the ones in which you could see their unique designs clearly. She waved Nathan to come to the booth. "Might as well be comfortable."

Nathan stirred his sugar into the coffee.

He watched the coffee swirl around and around like a miniature typhoon. He was unsure why he was there. It just felt good. He looked up and saw Sarah staring off at the falling snow. "Penny for your thoughts."

Sarah was embarrassed at being caught daydreaming. "Just foolishness. An old woman remembering long ago. I remember my Mama telling me that each snowflake has its unique design, no two alike and people are the same way — unique, and each of us has our own snowflake to finish. But that was a long time ago. Funny how I can remember that so clear like it was yesterday and I can't even remember where I put my hairbrush ten minutes ago."

"Maybe we remember what's important."

"You are a charmer, Nathan." She put her hand on his and patted it. Again, she saw the lost boy in him. Trying to get close to someone, his eyes seemed to plead for caring. Yet, she found herself wanting to be close to him. She wanted to share her feelings and tell him stories that were precious only to her.

"You have someone, Sarah? I mean are you married? Children?" He took a sip of coffee and listened to Sarah's rough voice. She told him of her marriage of over thirty years. Her husband was nearly fifteen years older and passed away eight years earlier. They had made each other very happy, sharing the good and bad together. They exchanged smiles as she told stories of his bull-headedness, chivalry and "how that man could putz in the garden." Nathan found himself envying her the relationship she had with him, a love that included a real friendship.

He watched as her expression changed, her hands folded as if in prayer. She glanced out the window and back at Nathan, giving him a weak smile. "We lost our son, Samuel, in Vietnam. How we missed him. Guess I still do. At least we could grieve together. I thought I would lose my mind, but Pa pulled me through that one. How that boy could play a trumpet! Had a scholarship to Julliard School of Music, but he never got to go. I think the Lord saw Samuel could play as well as Gabriel himself, and wanted him to play that sweet music just for him. You believe in heaven, don't you Nathan?"

He squeezed her hand and smiled. "I'm beginning to, Sarah. I'm beginning to."

"But twenty two years is too short of a life. Far too short." She grabbed a napkin and wiped tears that started to overflow from the rim of her eyes.

"It is too short."

"Children can hurt you in so many ways. Our daughter is named Angela. Such a child she is! She was the perfect little girl and smart as a whip. Then after Samuel — " Tears now flowed down her cheeks. She told of how her daughter quit after Samuel's death, shutting herself off from everyone in her grief. Angela had turned to drugs, doing anything for a place to sleep, and then just disappeared. "She didn't even come home for her own father's funeral. I still pray for her, and when I think of her I think of the little girl." She took a deep breath. She felt good about being able to talk about her feelings but needed space from it for now. She also knew the boy sitting across from her had his own story, sad as her's, but her's only had moments of sadness in what she felt had been a good life. She had watched his eyes moisten as she talked and now wanted to return the caring. "Enough about me. What about you, Nathan?"

As Nathan thought of his life he felt there really wasn't much to say but by saying it he thought maybe he could find it. "My mom died when I was born so I only knew her through pictures and what my dad told me." He remembered his dad telling him how much his mom wanted a child and risked her life to have one. Even so, he had always felt guilty for his mom's death, and without even thinking of it shut himself off from getting close to anyone in fear of further incrimination and loss. Everyone except his dad, that is. "Dad raised me. We were really close and did everything together. He was great."

Sarah could see him struggle with the emotions his words generated. "So, your dad never remarried?"

"No, Sarah. I don't think it was ever a consideration with him. He loved my mom so much that her memory was enough. I also think he wanted my memory of her unblurred. You know what I mean?" He saw her nod as she waited for him to continue.

"He died three years ago." Nathan, of course, didn't count the seven years he had been a ghost. "He's the best part of me. He taught me to be a man of your word, respect your elders, laugh at yourself, and not take life too seriously. I forget how much I miss him. He was my best friend." Then it struck him, like an electrical shock through his body. He remembered! He and his dad had been fishing. They were lying out in the boat relaxing in the June sun. The fish were polite enough not to bother them by biting on the baits. His dad had been talking about his concern for Nathan's inability or lack of desire to form close ties with anyone. Nathan knew now that his father had known about the cancer as he spoke those words. His memory, like Sarah's, was as vivid as if it happened yesterday. His dad, sitting up, placed his hand on Nathan's knee. Nathan shaded his eyes with his hand so he could look up at his dad. He remembered the soft rocking of the boat and his dad's words, "Nathan, you'll have a full life if you have five good friends. Real friends that are a part of your life." Nathan had laughed at the time and asked if his father counted as friend. His dad also laughed and said yes, he counted. So Nathan had flippantly replied, "I only have four to go!"

"You all right, Nathan? You suddenly went pale. Boy, with you I didn't think that was possible. To get paler, that is." The concern showed on her face.

"I'm fine, Sarah. Well, now I am. Just thinking about how precious time is."

"You bet it is. Can I ask you something personal?"

"Sure. Fire away."

"You have anyone special in your life right now?

"Just you, Sarah."

"You know what I mean."

His next thought was of Megan. But it was too soon, so he said, "No, not really."

"That settles it. You can do me a big favor. Now you hear me out. I belong to the Pentecostal Church, and this time of year everyone in the congregation becomes a do-gooder. Being a widow and all makes me a prime target. The Ladies Auxiliary, lead by Miz Alicia King done brought me a twenty five pound turkey and all the fixin's. Now what they thinkin' about bringin' a widow that much turkey, I don't know. Miz Alicia thinks the good Lord himself made her congregation monitor. See, if she gets wind that I'd been fixin' the turkey for myself, which I wouldn't, she would have half the congregation over to my place to spend Christmas with me. Now, no one should have to interrupt their family Christmas for Sarah. Christmas is for family, for close friends. You see my dilemma? I've already invited this young couple across the street. They got a new baby. But, you see Nathan, I sure would appreciate it if you'd come over too. It would make it real special. What do you say?"

He wanted to say yes, but by dinner time tomorrow, he might be out of time. He didn't want to break his word to Sarah. Her eyes told him a "no" would bring on an argument and he thought she probably didn't lose many of those. "I can't promise, Sarah. I'll try. I really don't know if I'll —"

"Now you come, and bring anyone you want to. The more the merrier. That's that.

You get wherever you have to go now and let me close this place so I can get home."

"Let me help."

"You sure like your punishment, don't you Nathan?"

It took over an hour for the two to close up. Not because there was that much to do, but because they enjoyed the conversation. Sarah locked the door. Nathan insisted on walking her home. If he became a ghost again while walking with her, so be it. He knew she would understand. She put her arm in his and they started to walk. The snow continued to fall and the night was quiet. They didn't talk the entire trip. They didn't have to. They reached her house and Nathan stood at the end of the sidewalk to make sure Sarah got in all right.

She heard the deadbolt lock slide free as she turned the key. She turned waving to Nathan. "Well, you know where I live now, 31 Sydney Place. Be here around four."

Nathan waved, putting his hands in his

pockets he started back when he heard Sarah call out.

"Nathan, tell me true now, these past years. The silverware thing. It was you, wasn't it?"

He couldn't help laughing. "Yeah, it was me, Sarah."

"Hmpfh. Thought so."

# Chapter Ten

Nathan watched the sun come up. He hadn't paid much attention to time before, but now he had little time left. Something inside him told him there was no arguing with the voice. He had started to form a plan. The clock chimed nine o'clock. Fullerton's would be opening in a half hour. Nathan entered the store and waited in the manager's office. Barton came in carrying the large contest entry box. He was short and overweight. His breathing was heavy from the exertion of carrying the box. He was balding with long black hair combed over the bald spot in an attempt to cover his barren top. He grabbed the microphone stationed in front of the one-way glass. "Dexter, how many stuffed animals were in the pool again?" He heard Dexter yell back, "12,344."

Barton started going through the entries. Nathan stood right behind him. He found 12,111 and tossed it when he came to 12,233. He continued the process close to a half hour when he came upon Chris' entry of 12,345.

"That's it!" yelled Nathan.

Barton reached up and rubbed his neck, feeling a cool draft. He continued his search and came upon Lori Beck's entry of 12,344. He tossed Chris' entry aside.

"There must be a mistake! He asked you. You said the kangaroo counts as two. You idiot, you have the wrong winner!" Nathan watched Barton rub his neck. He turned to find the source of the draft, not knowing he was nose to nose with Nathan.

Nathan reached down and returned Chris' entry to the desk. "The kangaroo, I tell you!" Nathan was holding it firmly on the desk.

Barton scratched his head, he knew he had tossed that entry away. He tried to lift it but it wouldn't budge. He looked at the entry again. Chris. Why did that name sound so familiar? He checked the clock. It was almost time to open the store. He stood up, satisfied that Lori had won the prize.

His mouth dropped open, his breathing stopped as he looked at the one way mirror. There, spelled in lipstick, was the word "kangaroo." He fell back into his chair. He remembered the boy named Chris now. He had asked about the kangaroo. "Does it count as one or two?" He had replied, "Two." He couldn't keep his hand from shaking. Things had become too weird for him the past few days. He reached for the microphone. His voice shaking as violently as his hands. "Dexter, check the pool for a kangaroo and if you find it, bring it to me."

"What, Boss?"

"You heard me!  Check for kangaroos!"

Nathan jumped up and down.  "That's my man!  You're no idiot, you're great!"  He gave Barton a hug and kissed his cheek. Barton snapped his head up and looked around.  He felt his cheek.  He was sure he had been touched.

Nathan reached the pool just as Dexter was coming down the aisle.  He could hear Dexter mumbling to himself, "Check for a kangaroo.  Why don't you come down and check for a kangaroo?  I'll show you where you can put the kangaroo  'cause I don't want any part of these things.  Something's not right.  Come down here and get your own kangaroo."  Dexter reached the edge of the pool and hesitated.  He poked a teddy and jumped back in case the animal took flight.  Nothing.  He smiled and approached the pool.  Out of the corner of his eye, he saw a stuffed bear glide from one end of the pool to the other as if it was doing the backstroke. He backed away from the pool and ducked as a teddy flew by. He was startled when his back rammed in a shelf. He swallowed a scream. The air was being filled with brown, blue, pink, black and yellow stuffed animals. He turned to run and was hit square between the eyes with a stuffed animal. He looked down at the beige kangaroo. He nudged it with his foot a few times to make sure it wouldn't take flight again. Without looking back, he grabbed the kangaroo and ran as fast as he could.

Barton took the kangaroo and put two fingers into the pouch. He pulled out a two inch baby kangaroo. How did the boy know? He looked at the two entries on his desk. Nathan blew Lori's slip and it drifted to the floor. Barton pushed his chair back. "Who am I to argue with that?" He reached for the microphone and looked out the mirror. Dexter was standing in a corner, his pistol drawn and pointed toward the pool. He jumped at the sound of Barton's voice. "Dexter, quit being the fool, and put that gun away! No one's been killed by a teddy lately. Get Herbie loaded, get the photographer, and come up and get the money order." Dexter reluctantly holstered his pistol. He walked over and slapped Herbie a couple of times to make sure he wasn't going to attack. Dexter either didn't notice there was a note tied to Herbie or he was still too shaken to care.

Nathan wondered how many hours he had spent on these streets. He had not separated one minute from the next, assuming there would be more. Now, knowing his time was limited, everything became alive, every minute thing was important. The colors were more vibrant, buildings displayed their personalities and sounds told him their own stories. He was like everyone else when he was alive. He never considered his time was limited. Why does knowing or not knowing how much time you have left change how you live your life? In the distance he could hear the laughter of children. From the glee in their voices and the high pitched screaming, he knew they must be sledding.

He could almost see himself on top of the steep hill. Looking down, he saw Minnehaha Creek frozen and, beyond the bottom of the hill, leveling off to the street. His father was laughing at his apprehension. The Racer sled with lacquered wooden slats and red lettering looked fast sitting there. His dad was lying on his stomach, his hands gripping the steering runners. Nathan climbed on his back, his hands putting a death grip on his father's shoulders as he kicked off. As the sled picked up speed, tears streamed from the corners of his eyes. Screaming in fear and excitement as the sled sped across the frozen creek, he could barely hear his father's laughter. Right before they reached the sidewalk, his father rolled them off on to the snow and the sled continued on. How quickly went the time of being young, yet how long the memories.

Again, he realized how he didn't let anyone into his life but his dad. Why had he been so afraid of letting others close to him? Friendship even then was precious to him but he would never risk it. It was more than just the fear of losing it. Maybe it was the fear of responsibility that came with friendship. Over the years he had convinced himself that being alone was more convenient, just easier. Loneliness had become an old shirt he wore comfortably. Now, he was learning that life is to be judged by relationships with others and caring about others. That was the gift he had been given. The time had come, the sky was darkening and it was time for dinner.

# Chapter Eleven

M egan's apartment was above the Ben Franklin store. Nathan stood in front of the apartment for the longest time. He was nervous, wondering what was in store for him. He brought his knuckles against the door and was relieved to hear the knock. Megan opened the door and greeted him with a smile. It was a smile that told him everything would be all right. She was wearing a green and red plaid shirt and faded jeans. They were accented by Christmas tree earrings. There was a freshness about her. "I'm sorry I didn't call, but I had —"

"Never mind. I knew you would come. Come on in. Let me take your coat. Hope you like lasagna. It's the only thing I make well. Not too Christmasie, huh?"

"Lasagna's fine. Just fine." He could tell that she was nervous. She spoke so quickly. "I want to thank you for inviting me, being Christmas Eve and all. I mean you really don't know me. It was kind of you, really."

She reached and took his hand, leading him to the couch. She noticed how cool his hands were. His face was pale. It was his smile and eyes that gave off warmth. "Nonsense. It was just as kind of you to accept. It seems foolish for both of us to be alone on Christmas Eve, doesn't it? I mean, somehow it fits, almost —" She couldn't finish, it sounded stupid even to her, but she had the feeling it was meant to be. It was no accident they had met.

The dining table was a wooden cable

spool. It had a red table cloth, two green candles and a formal setting for two. She lit the candles and turned out the rest of the lights. The smell of the lasagna, garlic bread, the glow of the candles and the Christmas music made the feeling of being strangers disappear. He watched her toss the salad. Behind her he could see the small Christmas tree with its twinkling lights and the few presents scattered underneath. She was like the tree — small, pretty and alone. He offered to help. She threw him a pair of oven mittens and told him he could put out the lasagna and bread. They couldn't help bumping into each other in the small kitchen. It all seemed so natural to both of them. They laughed at their small collisions, his reaction to the hot bread by tossing it into the air as he went, her humming along with the Christmas songs and the sounds of pleasure at seeing the food.

They talked very little during the meal. The silence was comfortable. He had forgot-

ten how much he had loved garlic bread —
the sharp taste of garlic, the salt of the butter.
He smiled sheepishly at her as he took his
sixth piece. She laughed. They laughed
about her determination to get her car out
and his falling face-first in the snow. They
cleared the table and he insisted on helping
her with the dishes. Afterwards, they sat together on the couch — she with her wine, he
with a coke. Neither had noticed the music
had stopped. She brought her legs up and
tucked them underneath her. They talked for
an hour, both becoming more comfortable
with each other, revealing themselves
through glimpses of their pasts. He enjoyed
just talking with her, watching her hands
move and her facial expressions. Everything
moved at once, especially when she had
strong opinions about something. He
couldn't remember having the strong ideals
she expressed. Maybe he had forgotten, or
just gotten used to a ghost's point of view —
a more pessimistic one. The people changed

but the situations remained the same. He wondered if maybe he had been a ghost when he was living. He observed life, came in contact with others but avoided really being involved with them. He passed through without leaving a trace of himself with others.

She realized she had been talking a lot, covering everything from the environment and Save the Whales to government corruption. And she knew why. She was running from her feelings. She could feel them like flood waters against a dam. If she let the slightest feeling out, the dam would break and everything would just pour out. His eyes were saying that it would be all right. She knew she couldn't hold them back much longer.

There was a long period of silence. "You want to hear something funny? My dad was quite upset when he found out I had invited someone over for dinner that I had just met and knew nothing about, just because he helped me with my car."

"He's right, you know, you don't know me. I mean, I could have been anybody or anything."

"Right!" She rolled her eyes and shook her head. "He didn't see you, so how would he know? Know how I feel, what I know. He's always thinking for me like he knows, but he doesn't."

He watched her face redden and her eyes fill with tears.

"I'm sorry, I didn't mean to — "

"Oh, it isn't you, it's just that — "

She went to the kitchen and brought back a box of Kleenex. She took one, wiping her eyes and blowing her nose she continued. "I went to the University for him, you know, my dad. I didn't want to. Maybe someday. Right now, I just want to work and be my own person. It seems all I've done with my life is do what my dad and mom want and that's difficult when you consider they've been divorced since I was six, each competing for my attention, expecting my favoritism. Can't they just let me love them?"

He knew what he had to do now, and that was listen. She didn't need advice. She just wanted to release it all. She told of the love she had for both of her parents, her feeling of failure in measuring up to their expectations, of feeling betrayed by a young man she had given everything to and the sense of loneliness. She didn't know what to do.

After everything had just poured out, she smiled at him and placed her hand on his knee. "Well, those are all my woes. What monsters are chasing you, Nathan?"

"Monsters? Funny, when I was ali— I mean younger, I loved horror movies, saw them all. But now I see even what made them really scary was when the victim was alone waiting or running. Things just aren't as frightening when you're with someone. Maybe my monster all along has been loneliness. But mine is different than yours because I chose not to let anyone be close."

"I feel we're getting close, don't you?"

"I guess we are. It's about time I learn to trust, care about others. I'm just seeing that a person can go through life trying to avoid the pain of losing someone special, especially a friend, but, when all is said and done, they won't have had any life at all."

"Well friend, we won't let that happen, will we. When I saw you walk toward me, I saw your sad eyes. They are sad, you know — beautifully blue, but sad. There was no way a person behind those eyes would hurt anyone. I know with all my tears, and sad talk this may sound stupid, but this evening has made me really happy. I'm glad you came."

"So am I."

She walked over to the small tree and reached underneath. She took the small wrapped package and handed it to him.

"I want you to have this."

"Megan, I can't take this. Besides, I didn't get you—"

"Nonsense. I hadn't thought before that I would give this present to anyone. It was bought for Mr. Right, who, as you know, turned into Mr. Wrong! But it just seems right to give it to you, almost as if I had bought for you in the first place. Know what I mean?"

He watched as a single tear fell on the small package. It was the first present he had been given since his father was alive. His throat tightened and an ache pierced his chest. "Thank you, Megan. I wish I had something to give you."

"You have. Now open it. You might not even like it."

He carefully took the ribbon, string and paper off revealing a black jewelry box. He noticed his fingers were shaking as he attempted to open the box. He lifted the cover. It was a gold ring, a pinky ring with a green stone veined with red. He looked up at her, she was biting her lower lip, glancing from the ring to him. "It's beautiful, but this is too much, I mean—"

"It's bloodstone. Supposedly when Jesus was on the cross, drops of his blood dropped to the stones below and forever stained them with those veins of red. And I don't feel it's too much. Besides, you'd make me happy by keeping it."

He slipped it on his right hand. It was a perfect fit. He put his hand on hers. "Thanks so very much. I will treasure this forever."

She reached over and gently kissed his cheek. "Merry Christmas, Nathan." She walked to the kitchen. She dished out vanilla ice cream and poured a small amount of creme de menthe on each. Grabbing two spoons, she returned to the couch. She handed him a dish and then sat across from him in Indian fashion. She just smiled at him as each ate their dessert. She watched his movements and his eyes. The sadness in them appeared to have lessened and for that she was glad. He took the last of the ice cream and felt its coolness down his throat.

"There are so many things I would like to say but there isn't time, but I was wondering — I mean, I would like to ask a favor of you."

"Ask away, I don't think I will say no to you."

"You're stuck here for Christmas, right, no plans for tomorrow?"

"That's right."

"Would you consider having dinner with some special friends?"

"You mean, you and I and some of your friends?"

"Sort of. If I can be there I will, I mean, I really want to, but it's more important for you to be there."

"Why is it important for me to be?"

"I know it's confusing, even weird, but trust me on this. There's this lady, Sarah, she works at Bridgeman's — "

"I know her!"

"Good. Well, it's at her house. A boy named Chris and, hopefully, a policeman named Robby will be there. You don't have anything against policemen, do you?"

"Not that I'm aware of."

"Good. You two will hit it off, I'm sure of it."

"What's this all about, Nathan?"

"I don't know. I just feel that it's meant for you and the others to be there."

"I'll be there. I trust you, and who am I to challenge fate? What time?"

"Around four, and could you possibly pick up Chris?" He gave her a weak smile, knowing he was asking a lot and watched as she gave him a sigh.

"Why not. But how—"

"I wrote him a note telling him someone would pick him up. I was hoping—"

"Right."

He scribbled down Sarah and Chris' addresses. "This should be a special Christmas. Thanks for everything, Megan. I really have to go. I still have to get a hold of Robby." He wanted to stay, he wanted to be with her. She was an elixir to him. Maybe all friends are, he thought. He felt anger at wasting his life, but now he had his chance.

"You all right, Nathan? You were staring off and—"

"Just fine. Just thinking how nice, great it's been this evening and not wanting it to end. But I do have to leave."

"Well, there's tomorrow."

"Right. There is tomorrow."

Nathan searched the streets but there was no sign of Robby. He had walked through the projects, across the bridges, along University Avenue and all around the stores. He wasn't sure where to go next, so he found a bench near the Commons and sat. The night was quiet. He heard a car door slam in the distance and muffled conversation. The campus appeared to be a ghost town. He laughed at the thought, right now it was a ghost town. It was then he heard the sound of static from a radio, the off/on sound as the radio changed from transmitting to receiving.  He could not make out what the voices were saying, but from the speed and pitch, something urgent was going on and he recognized the voice transmitting as Robby's. He estimated Robby was probably three blocks from him.  Nathan ran quickly through buildings, taking the most direct route.  He stopped, exiting a building on to Main Street.  The stores were all closed.  The only sign of life was the flickering of small neon lights.  He saw a shadow across the street.  He ran toward it and as he closed the distance he realized it was Robby.  Watching his movements, Nathan realized Robby was being cautious, staying in the shadows when he could.  He had his gun drawn.

Robby had both hands on his pistol; the barrel pointed skyward.  His back was against the window of a storefront.  He slid forward.  Even in the cold,  his hands were sweating on the handle.  The Team Electronics store was the next building.  Its silent alarm had gone off.  He cursed himself for

volunteering to work the holidays. He
calmed himself by rationalizing. It probably
was another false alarm. Probably a falling
box, an electrical short or a mouse. He kept
his eyes looking into the dark, making sure
they had adjusted before entering the storage
area. He didn't want to give an intruder the
advantage of sight over his temporary blind-
ness. His mouth went dry and a lump hung
in his throat. His hand turned the door
handle. It gave way and the door opened.
He knew it was no mouse that unlocked the
door. When he entered, he squatted down to
prevent his silhouette from appearing in the
doors and window. He wasn't going to be an
easy target. The hair on his neck and arms
stood on end. His breathing came in short
shallow gasps. He sensed it; someone was
there. He heard and saw nothing, but he
could feel the eyes staring at him. He forced
himself forward. He slid his finger over the
trigger. Sweat ran down his cheeks and nose,
his mouth filled with the taste of salt. He re-

alized that he was blocking the only exit and that there would be a confrontation between him and whoever was on the other side of the darkness.

Nathan was worried. Robby had been in the store ten minutes. It surprised him how human time had become to him. He could wait no longer. He crossed the street, intending to enter the same way Robby had. When he got to the door, his hand did not grip the door handle as he expected; it passed right through. He was still a ghost. Nathan's mind ran through the implications of this and all lead to the same conclusion. Robby was not alone and most likely in danger. Nathan stared into the building. His only thought was he had to help him. He decided to go to the center of the building where he could better survey the situation.

He passed through rows of televisions, past the service counter and finally stood in the first aisle. To his right, he could hear Robby making his way toward the far end of the store. Nathan was two aisles over. Robby's shoes crushed small pieces of dirt. The sound echoed like walnuts being cracked. Nathan sensed the tension, a mixture of fear and flowing adrenaline. Movement to the left caught his eye. He moved toward where he saw it. As he got closer, he spotted a pale circle. As he approached, the circle turned into a young face. The youth's face was drenched in sweat. His eyes were staring into the darkness, attempting to focus on the sound of approaching feet. He was kneeling alongside boxes of stereo equipment and a small color TV. He was dressed in an old fatigue jacket and jeans and looked no older than seventeen. It was when the boy adjusted his position that Nathan saw the gun. It looked so large in the boy's hand. The dark gray metal glistened from the boy's sweat. Nathan felt that the boy was either standing his ground or afraid to move. There was a crash, and the boy instantly aimed in the direction of the noise.

## Nathan's Christmas

Robby cursed under his breath for knocking over the tray of tapes. Whoever was in here had him pinpointed now. The most he could do was slide over to the other side of the aisle. His heart was pounding. It felt as if it would break out of his chest at any moment. He saw there was only another sixty feet to the end of the aisle. He stopped, wiping his hands on his pants. He slowed his breathing and listened. Nothing. Whoever was there was holding fast and would have to be flushed out. He took a deep breath and started forward.

Nathan was so intent on watching the boy, he hadn't noticed how close Robby had come. He watched the boy begin to stand. He was aiming. It was then he saw Robby making his way toward the boy. He knew he had to do something, but it was as if he were watching two trains collide. Robby's gun was still pointing upward. The boy raised his arm. It was shaking. He started to squeeze the trigger. Nathan realized that the boy in his fear would kill to escape. With all his intensity, Nathan jumped in between the two, screaming, "No!"

The scream caused Robby to jump back. He lowered his arm and took aim. A figure jumped into the center of the aisle and stood. Another figure to the left started to rise. A blast rang out and for an instant the area lit up from the shot that was fired. He saw the first figure crash into the displays. Clearly the shot had hit him dead center. He lay motionless amid the fallen merchandise. Robby swung his pistol around to the figure that had fired the shot. He heard a pistol drop and the metallic sound as it hit the floor. The figure started to run down the aisle toward the front door, his silhouette clearly visible. Robby raised his pistol and aimed, his finger squeezed the trigger as he aimed for the center of the back. He stopped. He couldn't pull the trigger. As the door flew open, he caught a glimpse of a scared young boy running for his life.

## Nathan's Christmas

It took him a few minutes to find the lights. He dreaded the idea of returning to the lifeless body laying in the aisle. As he turned the corner and saw the scene, he stopped. His legs became weak, his mouth dropped open and he felt the blood draining from his head. He grabbed a pillar to hold himself up. He recognized the young man instantly. It was Nathan. He was sitting up dusting the debris and broken glass off his jacket. Robby could clearly see where the bullet had hit him. A round black hole in the jacket showed that Nathan had been hit in the chest. He looked down on the floor and there lay the .45 caliber pistol. He glanced from the pistol back to Nathan who smiled at him. Robby's legs could no longer hold him. He slid to the ground, his back leaning against the pillar.

Nathan stood up. He could see that Robby was shocked and confused. When he had jumped into the aisle he knew that both the boy and Robby could see him, he had willed it. Then the boy had fired. Nathan had felt the bullet hit, not pain but an immense thrust had thrown him into the display. He had watched from there. He walked over to where Robby was sitting and staring at him.

"I'm sorry about the dramatics, but the boy was so scared. I thought he was really going to shoot you." He saw Robby nod his head. "I'm glad you didn't pull the trigger, he was just a boy. And after this evening, I think his stealing days are over." He reached down to help Robby up but Robby waved him off.

"You're him, aren't you, the boy who died in my arms?" Robby's words came out in a whisper. He couldn't find the breath to speak normally.

"Yes, I am."

"But how could—"

"I'm not quite sure myself, Robby. All these years I've been here, a ghost. It's just these last two days anyone could really see me."

Robby shook his head violently. He forced himself to stand, backing away from Nathan's offer of help. "No, this isn't happening. It's some kind of sick joke. I mean, I just don't go around talking to ghosts."

"I see. Can you explain this?" Nathan put his finger through the bullet hole, then opened his shirt to show there wasn't even a scratch. "Remember when you told me the story of when I was hit by the car? The one thing you didn't tell me was that you hugged me to your chest. You were crying and said, 'I'm sorry, I'm sorry.'"

Robby reached for the pillar again, his legs were becoming rubbery. Robby couldn't help but reach out and touch Nathan to make sure he was real. Nathan only nodded. Whoever or whatever he was, he had saved Robby's life, but why or how? "I was wondering. How come you were in the store when everything went down? I mean, you don't hang out at Team Electronics, right?

Did you know this was going to happen?"

Nathan was staring at the ground as they walked. He glanced up at Robby as he answered the questions. "I'm only a ghost. I don't know the future." But he knew that Robby was involved in his. "Maybe I was supposed to be here. I don't know. What I do know is that somehow you and some others are involved with me, that certain things are meant to happen and maybe saving your life was one of them."

"That still doesn't explain why you were in the store."

"Actually, I was looking for you. First I heard your radio then I saw you go in. I waited, got worried and then I went in."

"So you were looking for me. What for?"

"I'm not sure, but it has something to do with loneliness and friendship. Are you lonely, Robby?"

The question pierced him like the bullet should have pierced Nathan. The cold air and the few snowflakes hitting his cheeks felt good. Once he started to answer Nathan's question, the whole story about the failed marriage, his son, father-in-law and his decision of whether or not to keep contact with his son poured out. Tears rolled down his cheeks, but it was the first time he had talked about it with anyone. He could see Nathan was paying attention, really listening to him. When he was finished he stopped walking, hearing the sirens in the distance. They had walked a good ten blocks. "So, I guess the answer to your question is yes. I am lonely and sad. Sad that maybe the best thing I could do for my son is give him up."

Nathan realized that most of the anger he felt was directed at himself. If he had only tried. Maybe this was his redemption, making sure Robby didn't make the same mistakes he had. "We all have choices, either you can do like me and fall into an abyss called loneliness, a blackness that devours you, or take the chance and bond with people, knowing you may get hurt. There are lots of people same as you, not knowing their choice, or like me, afraid." Then he thought of his dad and what he had meant to him.

The anger resurfaced and he directed it at Robby this time. Robby backed away from the heat of his words. "Give him up? Can anyone give him what you can? Can anyone explain to him what happened tonight, why you didn't pull the trigger, why you gave that boy a chance at life? What you feel for him right now?"

Robby dropped his head. He didn't try to hide the tears. "I just want the best for him, for him to be happy."

Nathan put his arm around Robby. "I'm sorry I got so angry. I just know how much my father meant to me. He gave me so much — caring, love and most importantly a friendship I never had with anyone else. Maybe what he gave me I failed to give others, but there's no reason you can't.

Robby smiled at him. "I guess not. It's

just hard. But this isn't all of it, is it?"

Nathan laughed. "No." It was time to tie him in with the others. "I need you to do a few things."

"I guess I'm not going to say no to the person — I mean ghost — who saved my life, now am I?"

"I hope not. I need you to go to dinner at 31 Sydney Place tomorrow. Now it's all right, everyone there will be alive. Sarah from Bridgeman's, a girl and a small boy and maybe another couple. Will you do it?"

"Sure, I guess so. Is that all?"

They started walking toward the sound of the sirens. "Robby, I want you to tell them the whole story. Each of them have their own reason to know, they will share their own stories."

"I'll be there. By the way, if I haven't said it already, thanks for saving my life."

"My pleasure. Robby, one last thing. I know it's late but could you get a Christmas tree?"

"I'm a cop. I can get anything."

Nathan stopped. "I guess that's it. I may see you tomorrow. I don't know. But I'll leave you for now." He started to walk toward the church. He heard Robby running up. He turned and they embraced. Nathan felt a rebirth in the hug. Maybe sometimes it is all right to be angry with a friend. Robby was his friend. Each felt the tears of the other then, without a word they walked away. Robby turned to wave, but Nathan was gone.

# Chapter Twelve

C hris looked down at his clothes. They were old, but they were clean. He had washed and ironed them himself. Herbie smiled at him from his place in the entry to the living room. Chris reached in his pocket and pulled out the note from Nathan. "Christmas dinner," it read. "Be ready 3:45 P.M. Friend will pick you up. Congratulations! Your Friend, Nathan." He looked over at his mother who had passed out on the couch, the glass of wine still hanging in her hand. He walked over and removed the glass, setting it on the table. He went into the kitchen, making sure everything was turned off. He made sure his note was taped to the refrigerator. He heard the knock at the door and ran to open it. A pretty young woman stood smiling at him.

"Chris? I'm Megan, Nathan's friend."

"I know." He slipped his gray jacket on and started to the door. He turned and grabbed the check on the table.

They started down the steps. A scream echoed from the house. Chris started to laugh. "Mom meets Herbie."

Megan put her arm around Chris' shoulder. His tiny arm came around the small of her back. It felt so natural for both of them.

Hands in his pockets, Nathan stood down the block from Sarah's house. He had mixed feelings about returning to the church. he was disappointed that nothing had happened, yet glad that he might have a chance to join his friends. He saw the red Mustang come around the corner and stop across from Sarah's. Chris and Megan got out. the boy waited for her. Nathan started to run toward them but, as he did, it happened. He stopped. He was fading. He could see through his hand, his entire body was translucent. He looked up. A blue Duster carrying a large spruce pulled up and stopped across from the Mustang. A young couple from a house next to Megan's car came out. The woman was carrying a small infant. They all gathered around the Duster, shaking hands and making introductions.

Looking out the window, Sarah saw the young people gathering around the front of her house. She knew they had come to spend Christmas with her. She grabbed her shawl and, quickly wrapping it around her shoulders, she ran out to greet them. "My Lord, we are having a Christmas today. And look at that tree! We'll have some digging to do in the basement for my tree decorations. It must be ten years since I had a tree!" She reached down and shook Chris' hand. "I'm Sarah."

He smiled. "I'm Chris."

"Well, Chris. Hope you're hungry boy, got a turkey big as you in the oven." The girl came up and, without thinking, they hugged.

"Sarah, I'm Megan, Nathan's friend."

"Of course you are, girl." She looked at Robby. "And I know you, you're Robby, the policeman."

Robby and Ted Sullivan started untying the tree from the car. Sarah's heart ached from the feeling of family around her. She took Chris' hand and started to lead him to the house. He stopped and stared up the street. She followed his gaze until she found what he was looking at. There was Nathan, hands in his pockets; he was barely visible. She knelt next to Chris. "I see him too, son. I think he was supposed to bring us together. Now his job is done, and well, I think maybe he has someplace else he is supposed to be."

She watched as Chris nodded in understanding. Sarah looked up at Megan. She had tears in her eyes and her hand was giving a weak wave to Nathan. She turned to see Robby, smiling at Nathan and giving him a wink.

Ted looked to where everyone was staring. "I don't see anyone, do you honey?" His wife shook her head. "Will someone tell me what everyone is looking at?"

Sarah stood up. "A friend, a very special friend. I think all of us will have something to tell about Nathan. She looked back and he was gone. "Well, let's get in before these old bones freeze. We have a tree to decorate!"

Nathan watched them go into the house. He understood that it was time to return to the church, but he had one last stop he wanted to make.

He was surprised to hear the muffled voices of Brian and Jim in the record shop. Brian was needling Jim. "I told you we should have stayed here and finished wrapping last night. Now we'll be late to Mom's. You never listen to me!"

"Well, excuse me! I forgot how many nieces and nephews we had. Why don't we just give them the key to the shop? That would just about do it. A record for each."

"Where's your Christmas spirit?"

With that, Nathan knew what he had to do. With the same intensity he used the previous night, he passed through the door. Brian was looking right at the door as first a leg, then an arm passed through. Then the entire apparition stood before him. It was him, the ghost. He tried to speak, but nothing happened. He was more shocked than afraid. He managed to say, "Pssst, pssst, Jim, pssst."

Jim was wrapping a cassette on the floor. "What are you pssssting about?" He looked up to see, and there was Nathan. He could see his brother through the — the word ghost came hard. He watched 'it' walk down the aisle into the record room. He heard the speakers come on, and the sound of Carol King filled the room. Jim glanced at his brother who had not moved. He realized both of them were shaking and jumped when the music started. The ghost came back into the room, apparently listening to the music. 'It' turned to Jim, smiled and said, "Merry Christmas, Jim. You too, Brian. Merry Christmas." Jim couldn't speak but waved at the ghost and watched it disappear through the door to the outside. They stared at each other for a moment, then they both rushed to the door, knocking each other down. They fought each other to get the door open. Finally, Jim pushed his brother into the street. They looked around but there was no sign of what they had just seen. Jim turned to his brother. Brian had his hands on his hips and was gloating at him.

"Well, Jim, now what do you have to say, Big Shot. Huh, Mr. Right?"

Jim turned toward the door. "Ah, shut up!" He walked inside slamming the door, leaving his brother outside pounding on the door, yelling to get in.

Nathan returned to the church. The coven of ice and snow was just as it was when he left. He sat on the stairway and waited. He stared at the ice and snow, as the blue light got brighter and brighter. A soft woman's voice spoke, "It is time, Nathan." A feeling of exhilaration came over him. He was filled with happiness as he stepped into the light. His thoughts of his friends went with him. And even though he had never heard the voice before, he knew it was his mother's. He disappeared into the light smiling, and then the light was gone. The church bells started to ring and ring.